The Whatif Monster
Chapter Book Series

♡ Michelle Nilson-Schmidt

Michelle Nelson-Schmidt/MNS PRESS
13430 Gulf Beach HWY # 132
Perdido Key, Florida 32507
www.MNScreative.com

Author: Michelle Nelson-Schmidt
Title: The Whatif Monster Chapter Book Series: A New Friend for Jonathan James/Michelle Nelson-Schmidt
Description: First edition. | Florida: MNS PRESS, 2019. | Summary: Jonathan James wants to make friends with Sam, the coolest and bravest girl in class, but he is too scared that she won't like him. With the help of his furry green friend, the Whatif Monster, and a clever game that helps them concentrate on all the good what ifs, we find out if Jonathan James is brave enough to overcome his fears and make a new friend.

Identifiers: ISBN 978-1-7326942-4-8 (Hardcover)
ISBN 978-1-7326942-3-1 (Paperback)

Text Copyright ©Michelle Nelson-Schmidt, 2019

Illustration Copyright ©Michelle Nelson-Schmidt, 2019

Book Cover Design by ©Michelle Nelson-Schmidt, 2019

Editor: Catherine Findlay

Text font is OpenDyslexic Regular.

Perdido Key / Michelle Nelson-Schmidt — First Edition

Printed in the United States of America

The Whatif Monster

Chapter Book Series

A New Friend
for Jonathan James

By Michelle Nelson-Schmidt

MNS
PRESS

Introducing...
Ta-Da!!!

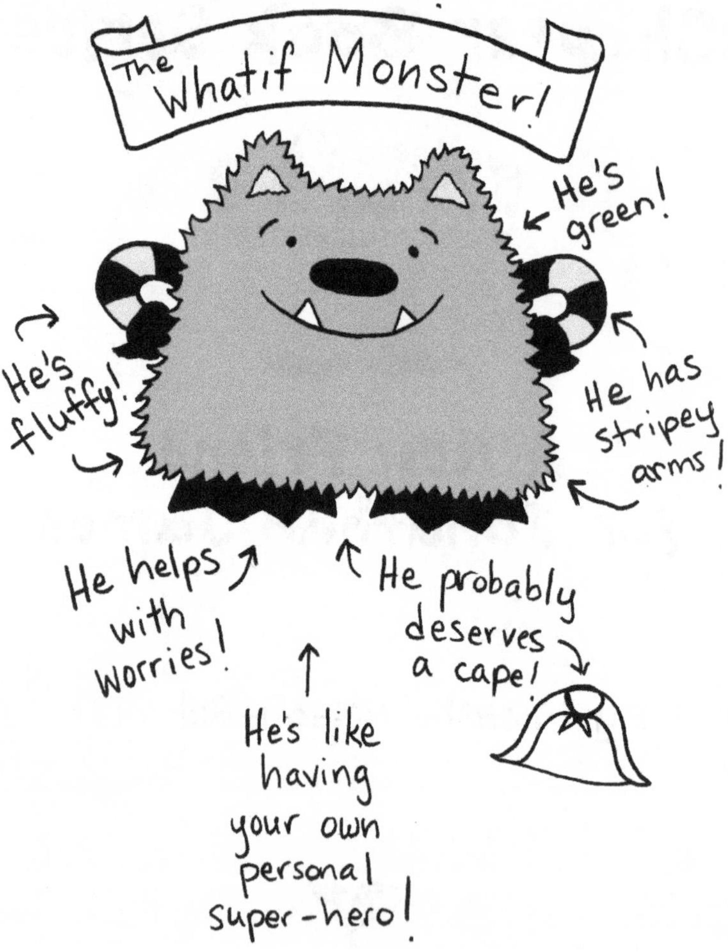

Chapter 1

Jonathan James worried about a lot of things. He worried almost all of the time. Luckily, he always had his Whatif Monster by his side to help him.

Jonathan James watched Sam standing on top of the monkey bars at recess. She was the bravest girl in the second grade.

"I'm queen of the mountain!" cried Sam. She sat on the bars, locked her legs, and hung upside down.

The other kids laughed and cheered. "Go, Queen Sam!"

Jonathan James stayed quiet but watched and smiled.

"Why don't you go over there and play with her?" the Whatif Monster asked.

"Are you kidding? What if she doesn't even know my name? What if she thinks I'm the goofiest kid in class? What if I walk over there and trip and fall down right

in front of everybody? No,

thank you!"

"I don't think any of those things will happen. I think we need to play the game," the Whatif Monster said.

When Jonathan James got to worrying about all the terrible things that might happen, they played the Whatif game. Jonathan James had to admit that it always made him feel better.

"Okay, let's try," he said.

The Whatif Monster clapped his hands. "Goody! Tell me the best, craziest things that could happen if you make friends with Sam!"

"What if it's the championship baseball game and one of Sam's teammates gets abducted by aliens? And what if I volunteer to play and I hit a homerun? And what if I help Sam's team win and Sam declares me the most valuable player? And what if the whole team carries me away on their shoulders cheering for me?"

"Oh, that's a good one! Kind of makes you forget about all those bad what ifs, doesn't it?" asked the Whatif Monster.

"You're right. I'm going to think about all the good what ifs and go talk to Sam!"

Chapter 2

Jonathan James took a
deep breath and walked up
to Sam. He tapped her on
the shoulder. She turned
around but had a funny
look on her face.

"Be brave," Jonathan James whispered to himself. "Hi, Sam. I'm Jonathan James, and I—" Just then the recess bell rang. Sam turned around and ran inside.

Jonathan James stood there alone. Sam had run away! He bit his lip as he tried not to cry.

The Whatif Monster ran up to him. "Well, what did Sam say? Are you going to play after school?"

"Leave me alone! I'm never playing your dumb game again!" Jonathan James ran inside.

By the time Jonathan James got back to class, he was feeling bad about yelling at his furry green friend. But then he saw Sam and he got angry all over again. He looked away. He couldn't believe he had ever

thought Sam would want to
be his friend.

He avoided Sam the rest of
the day. It was the longest
day of school ever. Finally it
was time to go home.

Chapter 3

Jonathan James packed his bookbag slowly as all the other kids left. He didn't want to talk to anyone.

He went outside and
walked down the sidewalk
to go home. The Whatif
Monster jumped out
of the bushes. "Hey!
What happened?"

Jonathan James looked over at his friend. The Whatif Monster had only been trying to help. "I'm sorry I yelled at you. I was upset because Sam ignored me and ran away," said Jonathan James.

"Oh, that is bad. I'm so sorry," said the Whatif Monster.

Just then they heard a voice

yelling from behind them.

"Hey! Jonathan James!

Wait up!" Sam was running

toward them.

Jonathan James froze. He

wanted to run away or

hide in the bushes. The

Whatif Monster whispered,

"What if you're brave again?

What if you can do it?

I know you can. Maybe
you'll hit a home run!"

Jonathan James took a deep breath and nodded. "Hi, Sam! Do you want to walk home with us?"

"Yes I do! I wanted to talk to you all day but I couldn't get your attention. I'm sorry I ran away from you at recess. I had to get to the nurse's office right away."

Sam had been trying to talk to him all day? "I thought you didn't want to be friends with me!" said Jonathan James.

"No! I think you're cool! I mean, you're really good at math, you have awesome hair, and you're the only kid I know who has a monster for a friend!" Sam said.

A giant smile spread across the Whatif Monster's face. "Think we can all be friends?" asked Sam.

Now it was Jonathan James' turn to smile big. "I'd love that!"

"Great! Ask your mom if you can come to my house after school tomorrow," said Sam.

"I will! Hey, why did you have to go to the nurse?"

Sam looked down at the ground. "I'll tell you if you promise not to tell anyone."

"Of course I promise," said Jonathan James.

Sam pulled back her hair to show a piece of plastic

behind her ear. Jonathan James and the Whatif Monster moved in closer to look. "What is that?" he asked Sam.

"It's a hearing aid. I have one for each ear. The batteries were going dead. I had to go to the nurse to put in new batteries. I had to hurry or..."

"Or what?" asked Jonathan James.

"...or I wouldn't be able to hear. I'm deaf and can't hear without my hearing aids. None of the other kids know, and I'm scared they'll make fun of me if they find out," Sam said quietly.

Jonathan James couldn't believe it. The bravest

kid he knew was scared

of what other kids would

think of her. "Sam, I

don't think you have to

be scared of telling the

class. As a matter of fact, we can teach you a great game that will help you be brave."

Jonathan James winked at the Whatif Monster, and the Whatif Monster grinned back.

Have more adventures with

the Whatif Monster!

Learn more and get lots of

free downloads at

www.WhatifMonster.com

Join the author every

Wednesday at 7:30 pm EST for

Storytime Live at

www.facebook.com/MNScreative

CPSIA information can be obtained
at www.ICGtesting.com
Printed in the USA
JSHW010822020120
3318JS00001B/73